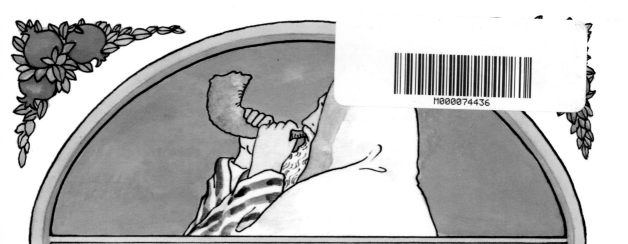

The ArtScroll Children's Holiday Series

①

Yaffa Ganz

ROSH HASHANAH
WITH BINA, BENNY AND CHAGGAI HAYONAH

Illustrated by Liat Benyaminy Ariel

HALOM! I'm Chaggai HaYonah — Chaggai the holiday dove. And those are my friends, Bina and Benny. I'm going to show you how they get ready for Rosh Hashanah.

Today is the twenty-ninth of Elul, the last day of the old year. In Elul, the shofar is blown on weekday mornings. And during the last week or so, there are special prayers called *Selichos* — asking *Hashem* to forgive us for the things we've done wrong.

All month long, Bina and Benny tried very hard to act a little better than usual. They gave more *tzedakah* and helped their mother more and were especially kind to each other and to their friends.

Now they are wearing their nicest, newest clothes and setting the table with the best dishes. Do you know why they are doing all these things? Because tonight is Rosh Hashanah, the beginning of a new year!

hen you say "Rosh Hashanah," what's the first thing you think of? The ram's horn we call a shofar!

The word shofar comes from the Hebrew word *l'shaper* — to improve. That's because the job of the shofar is to help us improve ourselves. Each time we blow it, it reminds us of some very important things. It reminds us of *Akeidas Yitzchak*, and of the sound of the shofar when the Jews received the Torah at *Har Sinai*.

On Rosh Hashanah we blow the shofar not once, not twice, not ten times and not twenty. We blow it one hundred times each day. The shofar, however, is not blown on Shabbos. So when Rosh Hashanah falls on Shabbos, we only blow the shofar one day.

There are three shofar sounds:
- ☐ TEKIAH — one long, steady blow
- ☐ SHEVARIM — three not-too-long-not-too-short blows
- ☐ TERUAH — a long line of quick, short blows
  (Sometimes, we blow Shevarim and Teruah together.)

Benny has been practicing very hard on the shofar, but no matter how hard he blows, he still can't get a perfect, long, steady *Tekiah* sound. Blowing the shofar can really put you out of breath! I tried it once, but my shofar only made soft cooing sounds. In fact, it sounded just like a dove!

n important days, we do important things, and when Rosh Hashanah comes near, there are three especially important *mitzvos* to do.

תְּשׁוּבָה —TESHUVAH

תְּפִלָּה —TEFILLAH

צְדָקָה — TZEDAKAH

Doing *Teshuvah* means returning to *Hashem* and doing His *mitzvos*. Bina and Benny want to be good Jews and good people and do the right thing. They are sorry for all the not-so-good things they might have done during the past year. Doing *teshuvah* will give them a fresh, new start for the new year.

They are busy with *Tefillah* too. *Tefillah* means prayer, so they pray to *Hashem* to forgive them for their sins. They ask Him to bless them with a good, healthy year. Everyone needs G-d's blessings ... even doves!

Tzedakah means giving charity. If we care about other people and try to help them, we hope G-d will help us too. Whenever Bina and Benny earn money or receive a gift, they put some of the money into their *tzedakah* box. Especially before Rosh Hashanah!

All year long we try to fulfill the *mitzvos* of *Teshuvah*, *Tefillah* and *Tzedakah*, but when Rosh Hashanah is around the corner, we try even harder!

n Rosh Hashanah even the food is special: Round *challos*, because the year is round and begins again as soon as it ends; apples dipped in honey, to remind us to pray for a good sweet year; and, on the second night, a new fruit so we can say the *berachah Shehecheyanu*.

There are fish to eat so that we will multiply "like the fish." And we eat the meat of a sheep's head or a fish's head so that we will be like "a head, and not like a tail."

And of course everyone wants a delicious piece of pomegranate so that our good deeds will multiply "like the seeds of the *rimon*."

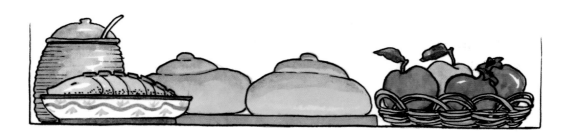

Bina's round *challos* came out looking a little lopsided and square, but Benny didn't laugh. He didn't want to hurt Bina's feelings, especially on Erev Rosh Hashanah!

Benny wanted to help make the *gefilte fish*, but when he mixed all the ingredients together, he forgot to add the fish! Bina didn't say a word. She just put the chopped fish into the bowl while Benny was busy looking for the big fish pot, and it tasted fine. I know, because I had some!

 e celebrate Rosh Hashanah on the first and second days of the month of Tishrei. Rosh Hashanah has several different names. Each one tells you something else about the day.

The name ROSH HASHANAH means the Beginning (or the "Head") of the Year. Although we count the Hebrew months from Nissan when the Jews left the land of Egypt, our year begins with Tishrei when G-d finished creating the world. So even though Tishrei is the seventh month, it is still the month of Rosh Hashanah — the beginning of the year!

The Torah calls Rosh Hashanah YOM TERUAH, the Day of Blowing the Shofar.

 nother name for Rosh Hashanah is YOM HADIN, the Day of Judgment. On *Yom Hadin*, G-d sits in His Heavenly Court and judges all the people in the world. He decides what will happen to them in the coming year. Will they live or will they die? Will they be poor or rich? Sick or healthy? Will they have a good year, or a bad one?

We pray to G-d and ask him to please judge us kindly and inscribe us in the *Sefer Hachayim* — the Book of Life — even though we may not always deserve it.

If we are perfect *tzaddikim*, G-d will inscribe us in the Book of Life on Rosh Hashanah. The names of the *reshaim*, absolutely wicked people, will be written in the Book of Death.

But everyone else — people who are not quite perfect, but not all bad either — will get another chance. G-d will wait ten more days, until Yom Kippur. If they are really trying to do *teshuvah* and to be better, He will forgive them on Yom Kippur and will write their names in His *Sefer Hachayim*.

OM HAZIKARON is the fourth name for our New Year. It is the Day of Remembrance, when G-d remembers everything we have done in the past year.

On Rosh Hashanah G-d also "remembered" that *Sarah Imeinu* was longing for a child of her own and He answered her prayers. Later that year, He sent three angels to *Avraham Avinu's* tent. One of them told Avraham that Sarah would give birth to a son in a year's time. Exactly one year later, Yitzchak was born.

Two other important women were "remembered" and promised children on Rosh Hashanah — *Rachel Imeinu* and Chanah, the mother of the prophet Shmuel.

On Rosh Hashanah, *Hashem* also "remembered" Yosef. For twelve years, Yosef had been locked away in prison. Finally, on the first of Tishrei, he was feed and sent to Pharaoh's palace, where he became the second most important man in Egypt. (Pharaoh was the first!)

OM HAKESEH is the Day of Concealment. On this day, many things are hidden, or "concealed" from us.

The other holidays — Pesach and Shavuos and Sukkos — all come in the middle of a Hebrew month when the moon is big and bright. But Rosh Hashanah is at the very beginning of the month,

when the tiny New Moon may still be "hidden" and not yet visible.

The new year is also still "hidden" from us. We don't yet know what will happen or what kind of a year it will be. So we pray that just as the moon is "hidden" in the sky on *Yom Hakeseh*, Hashem will cover up and "conceal" all of our sins and inscribe us in His Book of Life for a good year!

 AYOM HARAS OLAM — today, Rosh Hashanah, is the birthday of the world!

It is the day G-d finished the Six Days of Creation. It's the day He created Adam and Chavah, the first two people. It's the day the world was finally ready and waiting for all the *mitzvos* people would do.

But on the very first day of their lives, Adam and Chavah disobeyed G-d. They listened to the snake and ate the fruit of the Tree of Knowledge. When they understood what a terrible thing they had done, they were very, very sorry. They prayed and asked for forgiveness. *Hashem* judged them, and although He punished them, He forgave them, too.

So Rosh Hashanah was the birthday of the world and the first Day of Judgment. We hope that when *Hashem* judges us on this day, he will forgive our sins too, just as He forgave Adam and Chavah.

ong ago, G-d gave a very strange-sounding command to *Avraham Avinu*. He told him to bring his son Yitzchak to *Har Hamoriah*, put him on an altar and offer him as a sacrifice!

All his life, Avraham had loved and helped and saved people, and now it seemed as though G-d was telling him to kill! All his life, Avraham had waited for the child Hashem had promised him, and now that he finally had a son, he was commanded to sacrifice him!

Avraham did not question G-d. He trusted Him and did as he was told. Yitzchak didn't complain or object either. He knew that Avraham would do the right thing.

But G-d didn't really want Yitzchak to die. He only wanted to test Avraham. At the last moment, just as Avraham was about to kill Yitzchak, G-d sent an angel to stop him.

"Avraham, Avraham!" called the angel. "Do not touch the lad! Do not harm him! For now G-d knows you fear Him and that you did not hold back your only son from Him!"

Then Avraham saw a ram. Its horns were tangled in a nearby bush. He caught the ram and offered it as a sacrifice to *Hashem* in place of Yitzchak.

This is the story of "*Akeidas Yitzchak*" — the Binding of Yitzchak. It took place on the first day of Tishrei, on Rosh Hashanah. And on Rosh Hashanah, we blow a ram's horn — the shofar — to remember. We want *Hashem* to remember the story, too, for we are the children of *Avraham Avinu*. And we hope that because of Avraham, *Hashem* will be merciful and judge us more kindly.

n Bina and Benny's family, no one takes a nap on the first day of Rosh Hashanah. Who can sleep when they are being judged in G-d's Heavenly Court?

On the first day of the holiday, after they have eaten their *yom tov* meal and davened *Minchah*, Bina and Benny go with their parents to the river near their house. They are going to say the prayer *Tashlich*. The word "*Tashlich*" means "you shall throw." They read in their *machzor*:

"And You, *Hashem*, shall *throw* all of the Jews' sins into the deep parts of the sea."

Then they shake out their pockets, just as if they were throwing their sins deep into the water where no one will ever see them again.

I'm going to stay out of the way and keep my wings dry!

"Do you really thing we're throwing our sins into the water?" whispered Bina as she shook out her pockets.

"I'm afraid not," sighed Benny. "It's only a reminder to try and get rid of them. Getting rid of bad deeds is hard work! They can't be tossed out so easily. But if *Hashem* sees we're serious about it, I'm sure He'll give us another chance. He can throw all those sins away — if He wants to — right into the deepest part of the ocean, so that no one will ever see them again!"

enny, do you think we'll be written down in *Hashem's* Book of Life?" asked Bina.

"I sure hope so!" answered Benny. "I've been trying awfully hard to be good this last month. It hasn't been easy, either."

Bina smiled. "It's easier than it was last year. Do you remember? Last year we had a big argument on *Erev Rosh Hashanah*. I spilled some honey on your new *machzor* and it was all sticky. You hollered so much that Abba came running in to see what happened! At least this year we didn't fight."

Benny smiled back, "Instead of hollering, I should have thanked you for wishing me such a sweet, sticky year! You know, it's too bad you didn't spill some honey on all those stamps we licked before Rosh Hashanah. They tasted terrible!"

"But think how happy everyone was to get our Rosh Hashanah cards in the mail. I liked the ones we made ourselves best of all."

"Me too," said Benny. "But if I ran the post office, I'd still make sweet stamps for Rosh Hashanah cards."

"And I'd send the mail by carrier pigeons," said Chaggai. "A pigeon would make a perfect Rosh Hashanah mailman."

et's practice wishing everyone a good year," said Bina. "It's such a long wish to remember."

Leshanah tovah tikaseivu veseichaseimu l'alter l'chayim tovim!
May your name be immediately written down and sealed for a good year in the Book of Life!

"It's not so hard," said Benny, "and it's only for the first night. From then on, until Yom Kippur, all we have to say when we meet someone is …

Gemar chasimah tovah!
May your final seal in the Book of Life be a good one!

"Benny, I hope everyone is inscribed for a good year, don't you?"

"I sure do!"

And to all of you,
from me, Chaggai HaYonah,
have a *shanah tovah* —
a wonderful year!

GLOSSARY

Akeidas Yitzchak — the Binding of Yitzchak

Avraham Avinu — Abraham our Father

berachah — a blessing

chag, chagim — holiday, holidays

challah, challos — bread baked especially for Sabbath and holidays

Chavah — Eve, the first woman

Erev Rosh Hashanah — the day before Rosh Hashanah

gefilte fish (Yiddish) — chopped, cooked fish made especially for the Sabbath and holidays

Har Hamoriah — Mount Moriah, the Temple Mount

Har Sinai — Mount Sinai

Hashem — G-d

Imma — Mother

machzor — holiday prayerbook

mazal — good luck

Minchah — afternoon prayer

Pesach — the holiday of Passover

reshaim — evil people, sinners

rimon — pomegranate

Sarah Imeinu — Sarah our Mother

Shavuos — the holiday of the Giving of the Torah

Shehecheyanu — the blessing said when doing a *mitzvah* or eating fruits the first time in a new season

shul (Yiddish) — synagogue

Sukkos — the holiday of Booths

tzaddikim — righteous people

Yitzchak Avinu — Isaac our Father

Yom Kippur — The Day of Atonement

Yom Tov — holiday